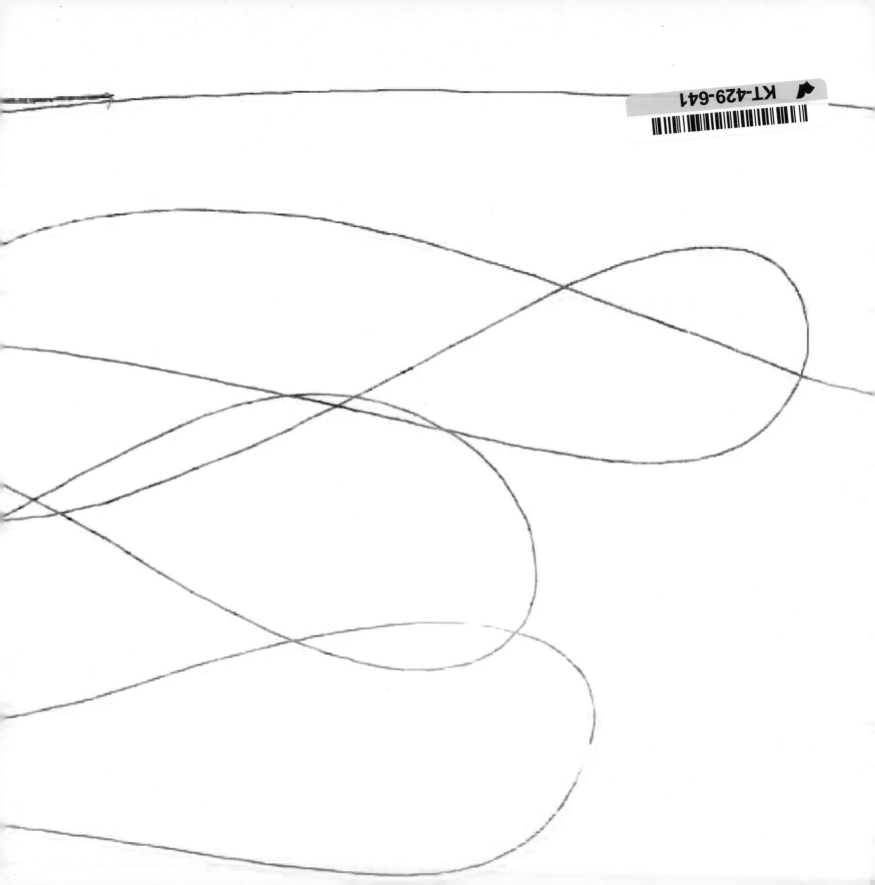

Contents

Introduction

Top of the Pops is called TOTP, Jennifer Lopez is sometimes known as J. Lo and Blue Peter is BP. In the same way, multiple sclerosis is sometimes called MS. When someone is talking about multiple sclerosis, and someone else is talking about MS, they are both talking about the same thing.

MS is just one of the many hundreds of different illnesses that can harm our bodies. Some sicknesses we get from other people, such as a cold. Other sicknesses just happen. They appear inside our body and sometimes doctors don't know why. One of these illnesses is MS. Doctors know much about what happens after MS has started, but they do not know why MS starts.

When we move our hand, or move a foot, it is because that part of our body has been told to move. There is one part of our body that tells all the other parts of our body what to do. It is called our brain. Without the brain telling the different parts of our body what to do, we would not walk, eat, drink or even play computer games. But how does our brain tell our foot to move? It does not have a mouth to shout out to the foot to tell it to move, and the foot does not have ears to listen for any commands. However, inside our body there are thousands upon thousands of nerves connecting the brain to every part of our body. The brain sends messages to different parts of our body along these nerves and once a message gets there, then that part of the body does what it has been told to do.

So the brain sends messages to all parts of our body along nerves. But nerves do more than just getting messages from our brain to different parts of our body. Nerves carry messages the other direction also. If we put our foot into a bath of hot water, the nerves in our foot would know it was hot and send a message along the nerves to our brain. The brain would then decide if the water was too hot, and if so, send a message back down to the foot along our nerves telling it to get out of the water quickly. Nerves are very important. Without them the brain could not send messages to anywhere in our body and without them our brain would not get any messages back.

There are many other things inside our body apart from our brain and nerves. For example, we have good bugs. They help fight sicknesses. When we catch a cold, bad bugs try to take over and make us feel ill. But the good bugs fight back and usually they win. The cold has been beaten and we feel better again. These good bugs are known as our immune system. They are there to protect our body and make sure it keeps working the way it should. But sometimes these good bugs do more than they are meant to. In somebody who has the disease called multiple sclerosis, they attack and damage nerves.

In the story that follows there is a river. Imagine the river is a nerve and the group of leaves floating on the surface is a message coming from the brain and going to the left leg. For the left leg to do what the brain has asked it to do, the message cannot be changed in any way.

The Plan is Hatched

Madonna lay stretched out enjoying the warmth of the spring sunshine. She could just hear the lapping of the water in the river as it flowed slowly across the meadow. A small group of leaves bobbed along the surface. But Madonna felt uneasy. There was something not quite right this morning. Her female instinct told her that, unlike all the other times she had been to the river's edge with the love of her life, today was different. Myles Stockingfeather was not casting his fly as often as he usually did and Madonna was not being petted as much as she would have liked. She knew Myles had had a restless night. He had tossed and turned in bed so much she had landed on the floor several times. He had even wakened Imogen, his wife of nearly fifteen years, with his grunting and groaning. At one point she had shouted at him,

"If you don't stop that snorting at once, you'll sleep in the spare bedroom in future. And you can take that smelly dog with you."

CHAPTER ONE

Madonna was furious. How dare Imogen shout at her master like that and then call her smelly. Madonna's coat smelled of the countryside; natural smells such as clover, freshly cut grass and, of course, the rabbit droppings that she had rolled in the day before yesterday. The smells from Mrs Stockingfeather every Tuesday after she had put on her make-up made Madonna wince and sneeze, and a corgi sneezing is not a pretty sight. In half an hour Mrs Stockingfeather's smells would have disappeared anyway. What a waste of time, thought Madonna. And as for noise? When Imogen began to snore it was just like Fergie trying to get going. And just like Mrs Stockingfeather, once Fergie got started, he was very hard to stop. But then that's what you want from a tractor.

As if by magic a small bubble appeared on the water's surface. Usually Myles would have cast his fly to this, as he knew a trout sucking down some food had made the bubble. He loved eating trout but, in all his years of fishing, had yet to catch even a sprick. Imogen bought the trout she cooked from Mark Zees.

"He must be a really good fisherman," thought Madonna.

7

CHAPTER ONE

Myles was deep in thought. The idea which he had first thought of in bed the previous night was getting more and more fixed in his mind. It was a plan that would make him catch fish by the ton, or so he thought.

"Move over, Captain Birdseye, I am about to become the best fisherman the world has ever seen. My plaice will be at the top and you have had your chips," Myles Stockingfeather chuckled to himself.

Myles had always been a dreamer, thinking up different ideas and sometimes even doing them. A small shiver ran down Madonna's coat every time she remembered what happened when Myles decided to make cider. This he was going to sell and make enough money to fix the roof over the bathroom. So Myles worked very hard for weeks and at last he had filled all the baths behind the house with very strong cider. (Years ago he had bought nearly twenty old steel baths at an auction. He hadn't meant to bid for them, but there was a very annoying wasp that just wouldn't go away no matter how many times Mr Stockingfeather swished at it with his rolled up pink newspaper).

CHAPTER ONE

About three hundred metres from the side of the house was a large shed. This is where Mr Stockingfeather's cows came twice a day to be milked. As usual, after their afternoon's milking, Jezebel was leading her ladies out of the parlour. They were going to a field they hadn't grazed in before and where the grass was long and juicy. The way to the field took them close to the back of the big house, past the baths of sweet smelling cider. As they got closer to the house, the smell of the cider grew stronger and stronger. Jezebel could resist no longer. She took off at as fast a waddle as she could in the direction of the smell.

Of course all the other ladies followed her and it wasn't long before they had drunk every last drop of the amber liquid.

The two young boys employed by Mr Stockingfeather, Tommy and Jonesy, had no hope of stopping the cows getting to the cider. Madonna thought that she could help and began biting the rear ankles of Jezebel, just like her great, great grandfather had been trained to do. But it was too late. Jezebel slowly turned her head and looked down at Madonna through half closed eyes, burped loudly and promptly sat down on her rather ample backside. Madonna managed to jump out of way just in the nick of time.

It had been a Monday and, being a creature of habit, Imogen had her weekly washing hanging on the very long clothesline. Madonna was now hiding under the oil tank and cringed as she watched Victoria, Emma and Mel blindly stroll through the clean clothes, collecting various items of Mrs Stockingfeather's underwear around their short horns. They staggered on towards the village. Miss Forbes, the chairperson of the local Ladies' group, collapsed outside the bakery when Emma, her head covered by a very large pair of Imogen's bloomers, mooed straight into her face.

The bathroom roof still leaked.

CHAPTER ONE

Mr Stockingfeather continued to stare at the banks of the river. His plan, he believed, was so simple, but would be so good, it surprised even him. He would dig out both sides of the river for a couple of metres, making the river wider at this point. This would make the water swirl around and around in the little bays he would create. He would then put some breadcrumbs on the water and, because the water would keep swirling and not go downstream, all the fish would come to this part of the river to eat. "Easy peasy," thought Myles out loud. "All I need now is a JCB, a couple of slices of Ormo, a big net and Bob's your uncle."

Madonna wondered why she had never met Bob. Did he have a tail? As Myles and Madonna left the riverbank a small bunch of leaves floated quietly past.

When he had put his fishing rod in an outside store, Myles walked over to the back door.

"Right Madonna, I'll open the door, you shoot in and I'll be right behind you. We can't allow her to escape." Myles Stockingfeather, as usual, was taking no risks. The 'her' to which he was referring was Mrs Stockingfeather's prize winning pedigree whippet. The name of this missile on legs was Sonia. When Sonia was indoors she was the cutest, most loving dog ever to have left her mark on any kitchen floor. But give her a sniff of the great outdoors and Sonia was off. She didn't mean any harm or even wish to cause any trouble for anyone; she just loved to run, and run, and run and oh, what's the word? Ah yes, run. And she was fast. Some say she was the fastest little ginger haired whippet in the world. Others who were more travelled said that they had seen one faster. She lived in England and was called Paula. They said Paula could run for miles and miles and at great speed (as long as it wasn't too hot).

CHAPTER ONE

All Myles Stockingfeather knew was that when Sonia got out, he had to catch her. Fortunately Sonia was eating her dinner out of her diamond-studded dish and nothing was going to disturb her. After Myles had finished his dinner of wild pheasant that Imogen said she had got from Mark Zees ("He must be a good shot as well as a good fisherman," thought Madonna) he waddled over to his comfortable leather chair and reached for the telephone. Ronnie, the local builder's digger driver, promised to meet Myles the next morning at the river where he had been earlier. Myles Stockingfeather then put his head back and within seconds was dreaming of opening his first fish factory at the back of his house. He could even store some fish in the baths. Madonna jumped onto his knee and within seconds was dreaming of a huge family get-together where she met her Uncle Bob for the first time. (Like her, he didn't have a tail).

The First Signs

Imogen Stockingfeather loved her husband dearly. She put up with his silly ideas, not because she thought any of his ideas were any good, but because it kept him from holding her back. Imogen worked hard; she kept the house spotless, she did all the shopping and cooked every meal and she also looked after the running of the farm. Mr Stockingfeather thought he ran the farm, but it was Imogen who told the farm workers what their jobs were each day, made sure the bills were all paid on time and did all the ordering of food for the cows in the winter.

In the last few months Imogen had been finding that she was not coping as well as she had done in the past. She used to love getting up in the morning and planning her day to make sure she got everything done. But now some mornings when she woke, she was so tired she felt she hadn't even been asleep. Sometimes during the day Imogen just had to sit down for a rest, something she would never have done before. She would laugh it off bravely by saying that it was a good excuse for a cup of tea in her old age. But Mrs Imogen Stockingfeather was not old.

CHAPTER TWO

Imogen had been to her doctor. It was just after she had started getting numbness in her leg just above her knee. She had pushed the pointy end of a sewing needle hard against her skin and not felt a thing. But it was the problem with her left eye that had convinced Imogen to visit Dr Gill. One Tuesday evening she was getting ready to go out to the weekly Bostock All Girls Society meeting in the village hall. Imogen loved these meetings. It was a great chance to catch up on all the gossip as well as learning about new recipes and the latest designs in cardigans. Sometimes guest speakers came and gave very interesting talks. It was the one time in the week that Imogen would put on makeup. Every time she did this, Mr Stockingfeather would say that she would have been better calling Ready Mix and getting the job done properly. And every time Imogen would laugh politely at his little joke.

First was the cleansing milk, which she patted all over her face and then rubbed off with cotton wool. At this point Madonna would hide behind the big cupboard in the corner, as she believed the fumes from Mrs Stockingfeather's make-up couldn't get there. Then the toner, the moisturiser and the blusher were all slapped on. This was how the lady who gave a talk at the BAGS meeting had told them to put on make-up. (When Mrs Stockingfeather had come home after this meeting, she had told Myles all about it. Myles wasn't listening but Madonna heard every word. The lady, Madonna thought, must be just like the farmhands because they worked in boots too). It was now time to work on the eyes. Leaning forward to be closer to the mirror she had propped up on the kitchen table, Imogen closed her right eye so that she could smear eye shadow on her eyelid.

Suddenly her world no longer existed. There was no mirror. There was no face looking back at her. There was no kitchen. Imogen quickly opened her right eye and everything she had seen before was there again. She sat back in her chair and blinked several times.

Suddenly her world no longer existed.

There was no mirror.

There was no face looking back at her.

There was no kitchen.

CHAPTER TWO

After a couple of moments she decided to try closing her right eye again, and again everything disappeared. Within a split second she opened it and clutched the end of the table with both hands. Imogen held on so tightly her knuckles turned white. So many questions rushed through her mind. Was she going blind?

Imogen didn't go to the Bostock All Girls Society meeting that evening. She didn't say anything about her eye to Mr Stockingfeather either, thinking that the problem would probably disappear overnight. Imogen just said that she was tired and had a headache and then went off to bed. Myles thought nothing of this as he had heard it many times before.

The next morning, after having lain awake all night, Imogen knew the problem had not gone away. She still did not tell Myles and, after he had left to get his paper from the village with Madonna tight against his heels, Mrs Stockingfeather rang her doctor. She was lucky to get talking to him on the phone. When Dr Gill asked if she could see anything out of her left eye at all, Imogen described that it was like trying to look through a window which was covered with porridge. Sometimes she caught glimpses of what she should be seeing, but these glimpses were like small patches on the window where the porridge hadn't quite covered. Dr Gill told Imogen to make an appointment with Mr Charles Good, the local optician. He would be better at examining her eye than the doctor.

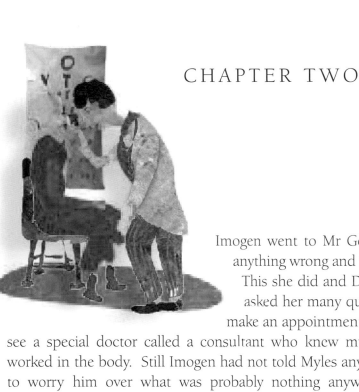

CHAPTER TWO

Imogen went to Mr Good but he could not find anything wrong and told her to go to her doctor. This she did and Dr Gill did a lot of tests and asked her many questions. He said he would make an appointment for Mrs Stockingfeather to see a special doctor called a consultant who knew much about the way nerves worked in the body. Still Imogen had not told Myles any of this; she saw no reason to worry him over what was probably nothing anyway. On the morning Mr Stockingfeather went to meet Ronnie, the digger driver, a letter came for Mrs Stockingfeather giving her the date of her appointment with Dr Sparrow, the consultant neurologist.

The Plan Takes Shape

"Come on, Madonna, today is the first day of our new life. We are going to make a fortune selling trout by the bath load."

Myles Stockingfeather was in great form as he strutted across the fields to the river. Madonna was even having trouble keeping up with him, her short legs having to take ten steps for every one of his. In the distance Myles could see the big yellow digger. Ronnie was as good as his word, and was waiting at the side of the river. When Mr Stockingfeather arrived at the riverbank he explained to Ronnie where he wanted dug.

"And why would you be wanting to do that for, Mr Stockingfeather?" asked Ronnie.

"I can't tell you that, Ronnie, it's a secret." Myles thought that if he told anyone about his plan, soon everyone would be doing it and there would be no fish left in the river for him.

So Ronnie did as he was asked and dug away a large part of one bank, putting all the mud, stones and even a shopping trolley on top of the bank. He then drove his JCB across the river and did the same to the other side. Myles Stockingfeather was delighted. The water was doing exactly as he had thought it would. Upstream the river flowed as before with the water gently making its way towards the sea. But when it reached the little bays Ronnie had made, the water began to swirl around and around at the edges. Tomorrow, thought Myles, when all the mud has settled, he would put the breadcrumbs in and start hauling the fish out by the net full. As

CHAPTER THREE

he turned around to go back to the house, a bunch of leaves came bobbing down the river. Instead of going on downstream, when they got to the dug out bays, they swirled around. A couple of leaves then went on downstream; another few leaves stuck on the bank and the rest just kept going around in circles.

Myles and Madonna went through the back door of the house in the usual way, making sure Sonia did not escape. Mrs Stockingfeather was sitting on the big sofa at the side of the kitchen. It was obvious she had been crying, as her face was all swollen and very red. Mr Stockingfeather saw this as soon as he had closed the door. He rushed over to her.

"What's happened, my dear?" he asked as he pushed Sonia off the sofa and sat down beside his wife, placing his large hand gently on her shoulder.

"It's my leg, my left leg. I can hardly move it. I was at the sink doing the breakfast dishes and I just fell. My leg sort of folded under me. I pulled myself back up and got over here. I've been here since just after you left."

"I'll get the doctor," Mr Stockingfeather quietly said as he rushed to the telephone. He rang Dr Gill but was told that he was out doing house calls but as soon as Dr Gill came back, he would give Mr Stockingfeather a call.

Less than five minutes later the front doorbell rang. Myles had just made a pot of tea and Imogen was looking less tense. He opened the door and there was Dr Gill.

"The surgery got me on my mobile and as I was in the area, I thought I'd pop in," explained the doctor. Mr Stockingfeather was delighted to see him, as he had felt quite helpless and hadn't known what was the best thing to do.

Dr Gill was brought into the kitchen where he asked Mrs Stockingfeather a lot of questions, some of which Myles didn't quite understand. However he decided to keep quiet and let the doctor work with his wife. But when Dr Gill asked Imogen if she had got an appointment with Dr Sparrow yet, Myles could hold back no longer.

"Who's Dr Sparrow, and what's all this nonsense about your eyesight?"

Imogen explained to Myles everything that had happened. She told him that she hadn't wanted to worry him and that was why she hadn't said anything before. Myles was annoyed he hadn't been told, but could understand that Imogen had not told him in case he would be worried. He decided it would be better to say no more about it.

Imogen told Dr Gill that she was to see Dr Sparrow in two days time at the hospital in Upper Bostock. She had been thinking of not going because the problem with her eye had gone. It had only lasted five or six weeks.

"Well, it's now even more important that you see him", said Dr Gill. He then turned to face Myles.

"Until Thursday, then, Mr Stockingfeather, keep your wife as comfortable as possible. She is not to walk unless you are at her side; she is not to attempt to do any housework and she is not to go upstairs."

When the doctor had left, Mr and Mrs Stockingfeather talked for a long time on the sofa. They had decided to move the bed from the spare room to the dining room downstairs and the table and chairs from there could go outside into one of the sheds. Tommy, one of the farmhands, could help Mr Stockingfeather with the moving of the furniture. When Myles got up and went outside to find Tommy, Imogen quietly closed her eyes and went into a light sleep.

Madonna had been lying under the kitchen table during all of this. She didn't understand what was wrong, but she knew that there was something not right with Mrs Stockingfeather. Since the time the cows had drunk the cider, Madonna thought that Mrs Stockingfeather had "put up with her" and had not loved her the way she had done in the past. Mrs Stockingfeather always gave Sonia her dinner first and if there were treats, Madonna was never given any. What Madonna didn't know was that when Mrs Stockingfeather had heard all the noise that day, she had looked out the kitchen window to see Madonna biting the ankles of Jezebel. Mrs Stockingfeather had blamed Madonna for the whole thing and even though she had told Miss Forbes that it was really the dog's fault, Miss Forbes had hardly spoken to Mrs Stockingfeather since that day.

Whatever Mrs Stockingfeather's feelings were for Madonna, Madonna couldn't lie on the floor any longer knowing that Mrs Stockingfeather was not okay. She jumped up onto the sofa and gently nudged in against the side of Imogen. As she was about to doze off herself, she felt a hand touch her head and then gently stroke the back of her neck. A pleasant warmth filled Madonna. The two ladies then fell into a deep, contented sleep.

CHAPTER FOUR

Fishing Put on Hold

The next two days were very busy for Mr Stockingfeather. He had thought about all the fish that would be swimming at his special place in the river but he just hadn't had time to get them with his big net. Anyway, his plan of taking over the world with his frozen trout fingers and battered trout fillets seemed unimportant right then. What was important was that Mrs Stockingfeather would be well again.

Once Myles had cooked his first meal, with Imogen giving him step by step instructions, he felt very proud. It didn't seem to matter that the boiled potatoes were still rock hard and the pork chops cooked under the grill had been on fire twice. He, Myles Stockingfeather, was now a cook. And anyway, the peas were perfect. They both had sat down to the meal and had eaten everything; Myles ate everything because he was so pleased with himself. Imogen ate everything because she didn't like the idea of eating Chinese carryouts every night.

On Thursday morning Mr Stockingfeather drove his wife to the hospital in Upper Bostock where they saw Dr Sparrow. Just like Dr Gill, Dr Sparrow asked a lot of questions. He also tapped Mrs Stockingfeather with a rubber headed hammer on her arms and all over both legs. He made Imogen walk as best she could from one side of the room to the other. After more questions, Dr Sparrow made a telephone call. He then told Mrs Stockingfeather that he wanted her to have an MRI scan and that one had been arranged for her in two weeks time. He would see her again a week after that when he would have the results of the scan.

Two questions had to be asked before Imogen would see Dr Sparrow again. The first was what was an MRI scan, and the second was, more importantly, what was wrong with her leg? Dr Sparrow explained that he thought there might be something happening to some of her nerves and that an MRI scan would take pictures of the nerves inside her body. If anything was wrong, these pictures would show it. Until he saw the pictures, Dr Sparrow was not going to guess at what might be causing Mrs Stockingfeather's leg to drag so badly, or what had caused her vision to become so blurred.

CHAPTER FOUR

The following two weeks passed very quickly. Mr Stockingfeather no longer burned the baked beans and his toast was no longer black. Mrs Stockingfeather was now learning to work the computer. She had found a program in one of the desk drawers. Myles had bought it but had never put it onto the computer. It was all about keeping accounts. It had only taken Imogen a couple of days to set it up so that she could organize all of the farm bills. Mr Stockingfeather had always spent at least a week and would say many bad words (mostly to himself) before he could sort out what he owed the taxman. Imogen did it in a split second, simply by pressing a button. Myles wasn't so sure that this was a good thing.

The MRI scanner was a big machine, much bigger than Mrs Stockingfeather had imagined. The two ladies in white coats who operated the machine asked Imogen to take off her clothes and put on a gown, which they gave to her. When she had done this, Mrs Stockingfeather lay down on a special table and was pushed slowly inside the scanner. About ten minutes later all the pictures were taken and it wasn't long until they were both in the car. Madonna was delighted to see them both when they climbed in. She had been allowed to come with them as a special treat and was even allowed to sit on Mrs Stockingfeather's lap while Mr Stockingfeather drove. On the way home Mr Stockingfeather drove over a pothole. Madonna almost fell off Mrs Stockingfeather's lap, but a hand was quickly placed around her, stopping her from falling. Madonna gave the hand a long slow lick. Imogen smiled.

Life had fairly much fallen into a routine over the last two and a bit weeks. Myles would help Imogen wash and dress and then walk beside her into the kitchen. The previous night he would have left out bowls, spoons and the corn flakes packet on the kitchen table. All Myles had to do in the morning was get the milk from the fridge. They both loved this simple breakfast because they used the milk straight

The MRI scanner was a big machine,
much bigger than Mrs Stockingfeather
had imagined.

CHAPTER FOUR

from the parlour. It was much richer and creamier than the milk that came out of a bottle. Sometimes they also had a couple of slices of toast with Mrs Stockingfeather's homemade jam A big pot of tea would wash it all down.

After breakfast, with Imogen seated at the computer, Myles would take Madonna and Sonia with him into the village for his daily newspaper, keeping Sonia on a lead. This morning he decided to go along the river before returning home. He hadn't been to his special spot since the day Ronnie had dug it out. He remembered that it was the same day that Mrs Stockingfeather had fallen when her leg gave way from under her. When Mr Stockingfeather got there, he was expecting to see fish swimming around in the small bays. Madonna and Sonia both stared into the water because this was what their master was doing. But they saw nothing either. Then Myles looked up with a smile and said out loud,

"Ha! No wonder there are no fish. I haven't put the bread in yet."

Pleased that he had found a reason why his plan hadn't worked, Myles was about to turn and walk home when he thought he noticed something different. Some of the mud and stones that had been left at the sides of the bank had fallen back into the river. The bays were not as big as they had been. "If that keeps happening," thought Myles, "soon there will be no bays at all."

Imogen learns what is wrong

A few days later Mr and Mrs Stockingfeather were back in Dr Sparrow's office. They were sitting side-by-side watching Dr Sparrow look silently at photographs.

"Just as I thought" he eventually said. Still looking at the photographs, Dr Sparrow continued, "Mrs Stockingfeather, you have multiple sclerosis."

Imogen and Myles turned and looked at each other. They had heard of MS. They knew that Tommy's brother had MS, but that was all either of them really knew about the disease. Both of them were confused. They didn't know even where to begin asking Dr Sparrow what this meant.

CHAPTER FIVE

After what seemed ages, Dr Sparrow continued.

"What has happened here," said Dr Sparrow as he pointed at several white areas in the photographs, "is the immune system has attacked some nerves. The nerves have swollen to try and protect themselves. When this happens, messages find it difficult to get to wherever they are going. In your case, Mrs Stockingfeather, when you had numbness in your thigh, the messages were not able to get back to the brain that you were pressing the end of a needle against your thigh. Also when you had problems seeing out of your left eye, the optic nerve had been attacked and was swollen. The messages, that is, what you were seeing, were not able to get back to the brain so that it could understand what it was that you were actually looking at. It got a mixed up message. Your brain read this message and thought you were looking at porridge.

You are having problems walking at the moment because you have had an attack on one of your nerves going to your left leg. The nerve has swollen and the message from the brain to your left leg has been changed where this swelling has happened. The brain has sent the message for the leg to take one step forward, but when the message gets to the swelling, it gets all mixed about. So, instead of the leg getting the message 'Take one step forward' it gets the message 'Drag the foot along the ground slowly'. After a few more weeks, the swelling will be a lot less and the message to your leg will not be mixed up as much as it had been. You will start to use your leg better.

As your nerve is healing it will leave some scars. Doctors call scarring sclerosis. On these photographs, areas of sclerosis show up as light patches, which we call plaques. It's just like if you have cut your finger. The flesh around the cut swells up

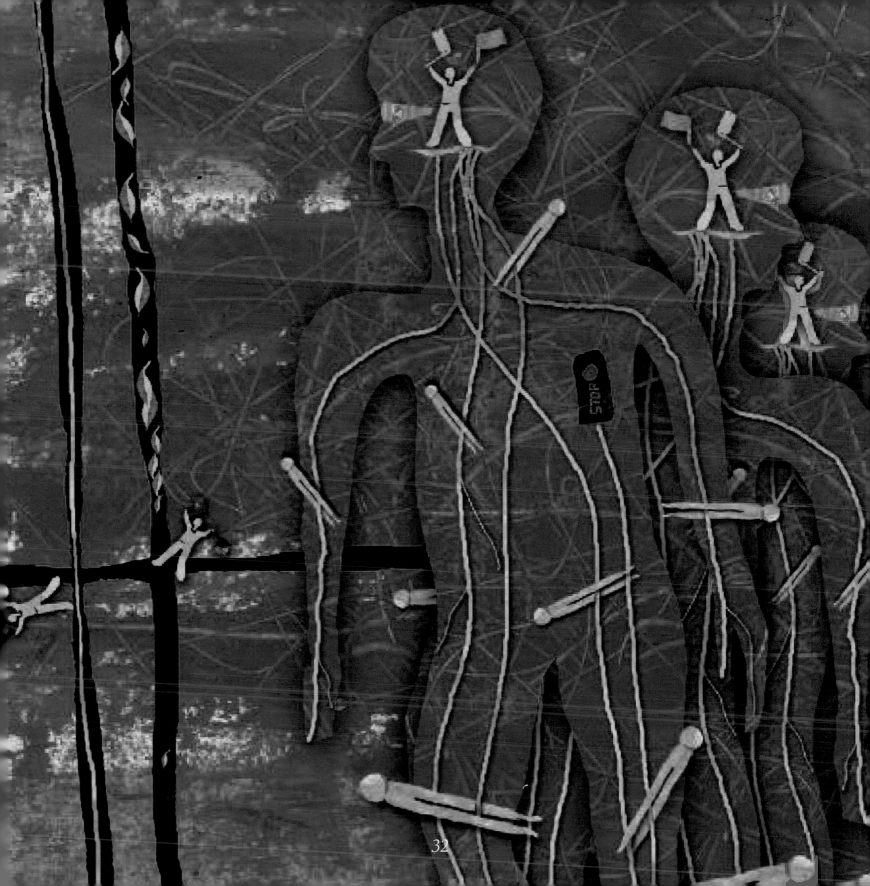

CHAPTER FIVE

in an attempt to protect the wound. After a while the cut heals itself but sometimes a scar is left."

Mrs Stockingfeather was finding it hard to concentrate on what Dr Sparrow was saying, but she thought she had the general idea.

"Does that mean that I shall soon be able to walk properly again?" she asked quietly.

"That will depend on how much scarring is left," Dr Sparrow replied. "The more sclerosis there is, the more likely it is for the messages to get changed. That's why we call the disease multiple sclerosis. Multiple, as you know, means many and sclerosis means scars. Many scars."

"Will that be it then?" asked Mr Stockingfeather.

CHAPTER FIVE

"Nobody can answer that question," replied the doctor. "Everyone who has MS is different. Some people have only one or two attacks. Some people have more attacks. Sometimes the attacks will be on different nerves, maybe nerves going to the hand or to the foot. Sometimes the nerves going to the voice box are damaged making it difficult for the person to speak. And then sometimes MS decides to attack the same nerves it has already damaged. As the nerves heal there is more scarring left and the message gets even more changed. There may even come the time when there is so much sclerosis the message does not get through at all. My secretary will send you an appointment for six months' time. I look forward to seeing both of you then."

Mr and Mrs Stockingfeather talked quietly together on the way home with Madonna curled up on Imogen's lap. Imogen was glad that her leg was going to get better and hoped that there would not be too much scarring left on the nerve. Myles was pleased also but wished he knew more about multiple sclerosis.

When they were settled back in their house Mr and Mrs Stockingfeather went to the computer. They found the web site of a local MS charity that gave much more information about multiple sclerosis than Dr Sparrow had told them. The charity also had a Care Line. That evening Mrs Stockingfeather rang the Care Line and talked with someone who also had multiple sclerosis. Imogen found this to be a great help.

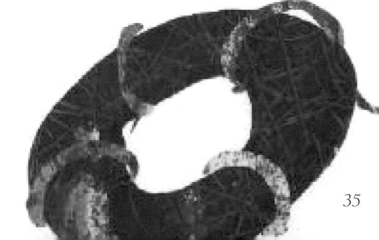

CHAPTER FIVE

As the weeks went past, Mrs Stockingfeather began to walk better. After a while she walked with only a slight limp and was very happy to walk around the house on her own. Mr Stockingfeather had much more time on his hands now, but he insisted on cooking all the meals at the weekends to give Imogen a rest. His pride and joy was Sunday lunch which was usually burnt roast beef with cranberry sauce, mashed parsnip and cabbage and crunchy (on the inside) roast potatoes.

"At least I'm trying," Myles would protest.

"Yes, very trying," Imogen would reply with a big grin.

After one of these particularly delicious Sunday lunches Myles decided to go for an afternoon walk. It was one of those autumn days when the wind was blowing strongly and the odd heavy shower of rain came from the grey clouds overhead. Mr Stockingfeather called both Sonia and Madonna and headed for the back door as he put on his coat. When he opened the door, Sonia took one look at the weather outside and dashed straight back to her bed beside the cooker. Running on a nice summer's day was one thing, but getting her paws cold and wet was quite another.

CHAPTER FIVE

Madonna wasn't going to let her master out of her sight. It wouldn't have mattered if there had been snow thirty centimetres deep (Madonna was only twenty centimetres tall), she would have followed her master anywhere, whether she could see him or not. They walked along the hedges, sheltering from the worst of the rain squalls. Soon they arrived at the place on the river where Mr Stockingfeather had thought he was going to catch all the fish. What he saw surprised him. The mud and stones that Ronnie, the digger driver, had dug out of the river and put on its banks were no longer there. When Myles got closer he saw that everything had slid back down the sides of the riverbanks and filled the little bays that Ronnie had made. A couple of the larger boulders had even rolled into the river and their tops could just be seen above the surface.

CHAPTER FIVE

As Mr Stockingfeather watched the river flow past, dreaming about his fish factory, a bunch of brown leaves came floating down the river. The leaves would have floated past without a problem but there were now a couple of large stones in the river. Three of the leaves swirled around one of the stones but then continued on their journey to the sea. They were almost in the same pattern as they were before they had come to the stones, but there had been a change.

"Maybe we'll try our plan again next summer," said Myles to Madonna. "Then again, maybe not. Who knows what the future will be?"

"Who must be a very clever dog," thought Madonna. "She has to be a corgi. Maybe she's my aunt."